A "BUTTERFLY HUG" LEGACY PAGE

TO: _____

FROM:_____

A Special *"Butterfly Hug"* Note from Me to You:

AuthorHouse™ LLC
1663 Liberty Drive
Bloomington, IN 47403
www.authorhouse.com
Phone: 1-800-839-8640

Published by AuthorHouse 04/15/2014

ISBN: 978-1-4969-0049-4 (sc)
978-1-4969-0050-0 (e)

Library of Congress Control Number: 2014905664

"Scripture taken from the HOLY BIBLE, NEW INTERNATIONAL VERSION.
Copyright © 1973, 1978, 1984 International Bible Society.
Used by permission of Zondervan Bible Publishers."

This book is printed on acid-free paper.

authorHOUSE®

Nov. 19, 2018
~ In Memory of Verlin ~
~ with Love to Karen ~
As you read + share this story
with your grandchildren may
God's Promises and
Legacy of Love
bring comfort to you all.
In His love ~
Beth Robbins Bontrager

DEDICATIONS:
Some Very Special "Butterfly Hugs"

This book was written from my heart for Children of ALL ages
who have dealt with the sadness & confusion when someone who is loved, dies…

"To God Be The Glory!"

"Butterfly Hugs" is dedicated FIRST to:
…..God & His Purpose…

*"For God so loved the world that he gave his one and only Son,
that whoever believes in him shall not perish but have eternal life."
John 3:16 NIV*

"Butterfly Hugs" is given as a Special Gift Lovingly Dedicated to:

Phyllis Robbins

Who, as a devoted Wife, Mother, Grandmother & Great-Grandmother
spent her lifetime loving her family
as she shared precious Legacy Lessons with all of us.

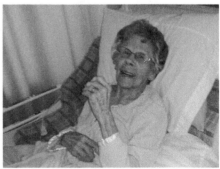

*I am grateful to God for a giving me a Mother who believed in me ……
and who ALWAYS encouraged me to never give up on my Dreams!*

Grandma and Becky Jo laughed as they watched the butterfly float on the air.

"Look at the designs on its wings!
God has made each wing a perfect match!
Isn't it beautiful?" Grandma asked.

Anytime that Grandma and Becky Jo were together God gave them teachable moments.

Watching the butterfly reminded Grandma of how life can change.

Grandma smiled and turned to Becky Jo as she

asked, "Do you know that this butterfly

has not always been a butterfly?"

Becky Jo had a startled look on her face.

"What was it Grandma?"

Grandma winked as she answered, "I don't

know if you'll believe me,

but it used to be a caterpillar!"

"No! It couldn't have been an ugly worm!"

Becky Jo exclaimed as she shook her head.

Becky Jo thought hard but she just couldn't imagine

that this butterfly could ever have been a

slow-moving, fat worm.

As the butterfly flew higher in the sky, Grandma

looked dreamily after it and said, "Just

like the caterpillar changed into a beautiful butterfly,

someday, we will also be changed.

The garden was filled with colorful flowers.

In the middle of the yard, a large oak tree

offered shade from the summer sun.

Grandma walked slowly towards the tree.

Becky Jo followed Grandma and they both sat down

on the stone bench under the tree.

"Grandma, will we become butterflies, too?"

As Grandma sat beside Becky Jo, she thought a

moment, "No, we won't become butterflies but I believe that we

will change from who we are now."

Grandma gave Becky Jo a big hug as she continued,

"Honey, all living things have a "cycle-of-life" which means that

there is a time to be born and a time to die.

For a caterpillar, its cycle-of-life includes being changed

into a butterfly.

When the caterpillar becomes a butterfly it leaves its old life

behind and begins a new life as a butterfly."

Grandma looked at Becky Jo as she tenderly reached for

Becky Jo's hand, "When we die, I believe the part that is alive

inside of our body, our spirit, will leave our body here on earth and

somehow we will awaken in Heaven in a new body.

We will leave our old life on Earth and begin a new life with Jesus

in Heaven.

I don't think we will look like the butterfly.

I really am not sure what our new look will be.

I just know that somehow we will be changed."

Becky Jo looked puzzled, "Grandma, how do you know these things?"

Grandma's face lit up with a smile as she said, "I believe in God's Word, the Bible.

It tells us that if we learn to know Jesus as God's Son and we believe what Jesus tells us about God and Heaven, we will some day live with Jesus in Heaven."

The sunlight was bright as a multitude of butterflies circled around them and landed on the flowers in the garden.

Grandma turned to Becky Jo and lovingly looked at her granddaughter.

Slowly and softly Grandma continued, "Becky Jo, there will be a day when I will die and I won't be here with you anymore.

When that time comes and you feel sad, I hope you will remember our talk today."

Grandma looked over at the evergreen bushes at the edge of the garden and saw that a butterfly was fluttering in mid-air. Realizing it was caught in a spider web, Grandma quickly got up and brushed the web aside, freeing the butterfly.

As Grandma returned to the bench, she said, "It is my prayer that as you grow up you will learn more about the many truths that are found in God's Word so that you will begin to feel the peace in your heart that I feel in mine when I think of Heaven."

Becky Jo sat closer and put her arm around her Grandma as she said, "But Grandma, I don't want you to die." Grandma smiled. "Becky Jo, dying is a part of life. We don't have to fear it."

As Grandma snuggled her head in closer towards her granddaughter, she said, "I don't want to die anytime soon because I would like to have many more of our talks as you grow up."

Listen, I tell you a mystery: we will not all sleep, but we will all be changed in a flash, in the twinkling of an eye, at the last trumpet. For the trumpet will sound, the dead will be raised imperishable, and we will be changed. I Corinthians 15:51,52

Grandma continued softly, lifting Becky Jo's chin so that she could look directly into her granddaughter's eyes, "Our talk today is an important one because if I would die without being able to say goodbye to you, you now know what I believe. I want you to understand that I will always love you even though I will no longer be able to be here with you."

Grandma looked up through the leaves of the oak tree to the blue sky above.
"When I die, my old body will stay here on Earth, but my spirit will go to Heaven and I will somehow be changed.
My new body will be made perfect just as God made
the wings of a butterfly perfect."

Grandma hugged Becky Jo for a long time then spoke softly,

"Today has been a very special day.

Becky Jo, when I die…I pray that whenever you begin to miss me,

you will just close your eyes and imagine my arms around you.

When you feel my hugs, at that moment, I will be sending you

Butterfly Hugs from Heaven."

Becky Jo looked up at her Grandma's kind eyes, "I love you,

Grandma".

And, with a tear in her eye, Grandma quietly said,

"I love you, too."

A Special Note To Parents:

Dealing with the death of a loved one is never easy.

Often we experience many unexpected emotions that can be alarming, uncomfortable and sometimes, debilitating. It is my hope, that as you and your family work through the grieving process, this book will in some way help open up beneficial conversations about a very difficult and emotional subject.

With today's technology, our children are growing up interacting with a "virtual reality" where they can manipulate results. Children who are used to this environment may have a challenge in accepting the intensity of emotions that they see and feel when they actually must face the true reality which inevitably comes with the cycle of life.

Children may exhibit many different reactions with some being subconscious cries for help to deal with their grief. For children, it may be doubly hard as they, in their limited understanding, may misinterpret what they see.

As parents, it is important for us to give them a basic foundation to help them work constructively through their grief. This basic foundation may begin by sharing your own belief system and giving them an "age-appropriate" explanation relating to the customs that your family follows relating to death. (i.e. Funeral Home Visitation, Memorial or Religious Services.)

Another very important component is to create an atmosphere where open communication is embraced.

I would encourage you to ask God for help in guiding you with His Wisdom as you seek to find resources that will help you and your family. There are many scriptures in God's Word that give both insight and comfort.

It is important that you NEVER be afraid to seek professional counseling if you feel that there are problems that you cannot handle on your own.

Sincerely,

Beth Robbins Bontrager

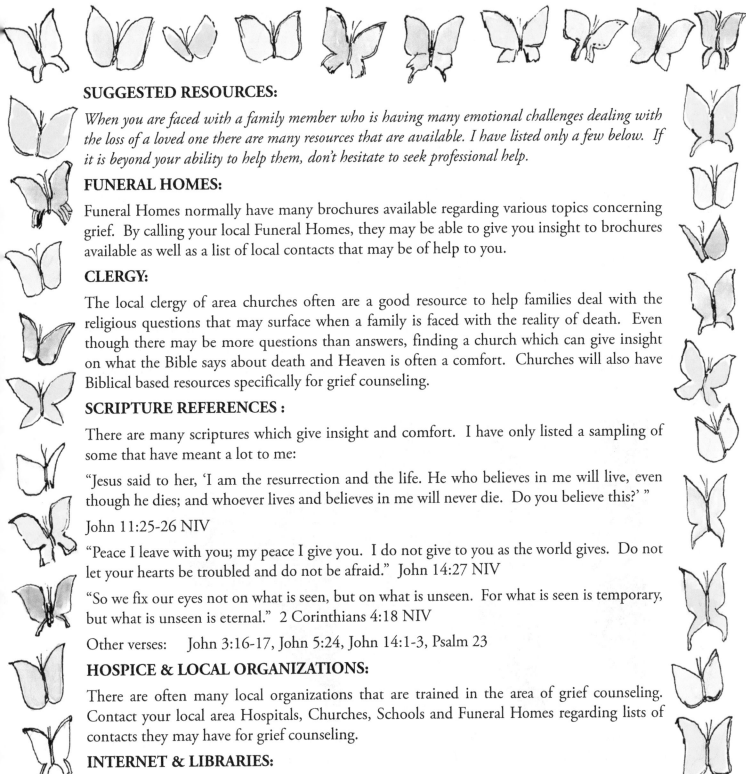

SUGGESTED RESOURCES:

When you are faced with a family member who is having many emotional challenges dealing with the loss of a loved one there are many resources that are available. I have listed only a few below. If it is beyond your ability to help them, don't hesitate to seek professional help.

FUNERAL HOMES:

Funeral Homes normally have many brochures available regarding various topics concerning grief. By calling your local Funeral Homes, they may be able to give you insight to brochures available as well as a list of local contacts that may be of help to you.

CLERGY:

The local clergy of area churches often are a good resource to help families deal with the religious questions that may surface when a family is faced with the reality of death. Even though there may be more questions than answers, finding a church which can give insight on what the Bible says about death and Heaven is often a comfort. Churches will also have Biblical based resources specifically for grief counseling.

SCRIPTURE REFERENCES :

There are many scriptures which give insight and comfort. I have only listed a sampling of some that have meant a lot to me:

"Jesus said to her, 'I am the resurrection and the life. He who believes in me will live, even though he dies; and whoever lives and believes in me will never die. Do you believe this?' "

John 11:25-26 NIV

"Peace I leave with you; my peace I give you. I do not give to you as the world gives. Do not let your hearts be troubled and do not be afraid." John 14:27 NIV

"So we fix our eyes not on what is seen, but on what is unseen. For what is seen is temporary, but what is unseen is eternal." 2 Corinthians 4:18 NIV

Other verses: John 3:16-17, John 5:24, John 14:1-3, Psalm 23

HOSPICE & LOCAL ORGANIZATIONS:

There are often many local organizations that are trained in the area of grief counseling. Contact your local area Hospitals, Churches, Schools and Funeral Homes regarding lists of contacts they may have for grief counseling.

INTERNET & LIBRARIES:

If you have a computer you may want to increase your understanding of how to help your family by looking up the issues you might be dealing with. Key words are important in finding the right information so it is good to "fine tune" your search criteria as much as possible. Be aware that if you put in basic terms, your search may lead you to some disturbing images. My suggestion is to use key phrases such as: "Helping your child deal with death" or "Helping a teenager deal with death".   Other phrases that can be helpful: "Scriptures to Cope with Death", "Children and Grief", "Teens and Grief". Local Libraries and Bookstores will also have resources that can be very insightful when dealing with grief.

Final Thoughts from The Author: *"A Real Butterfly Hug!"*

As I wrote this book, I often looked for little encouragements to keep me motivated.

In September of 2012 while I was selecting some landscaping plants for our home, I received an unexpected Blessing when I received a *"REAL"* Butterfly Hug....

The sales person who was helping me noticed that I had a Butterfly on my arm.
We laughed and admired the Butterfly.

Because I had been working on this story, I knew I had to try to capture the moment so I asked her to take this picture. As I explained why I wanted a picture, we shared a "moment in time" and both enjoyed a real *"Butterfly Hug"* instead of brushing it aside so we could hurry along with our day.

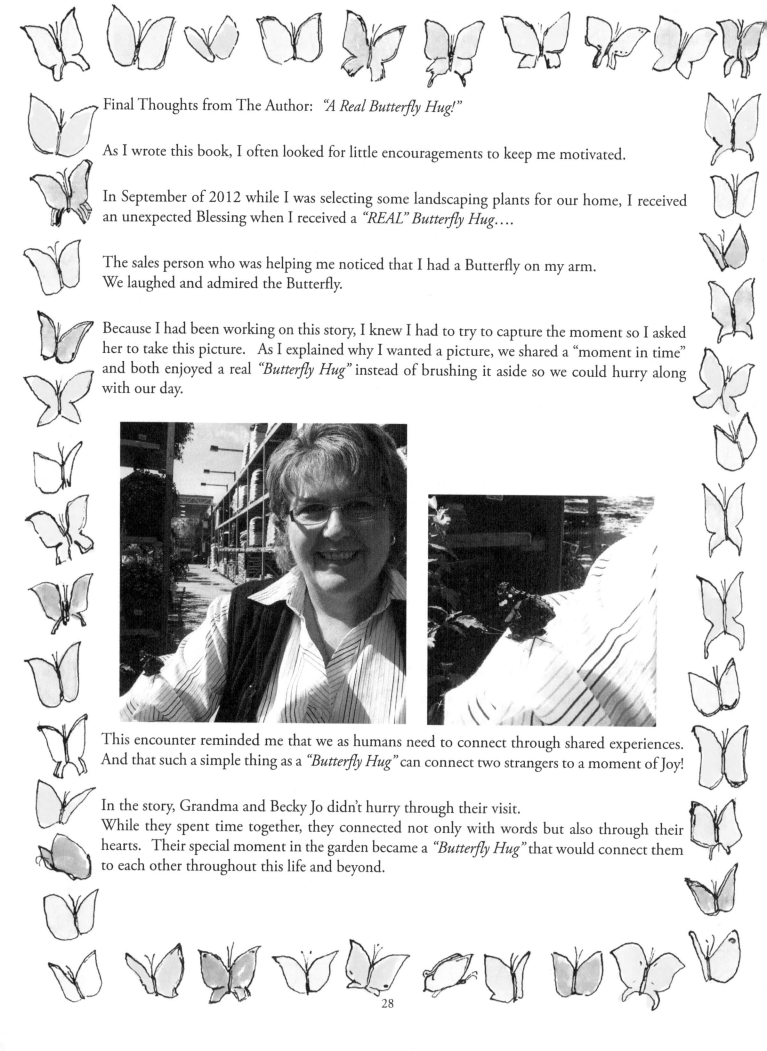

This encounter reminded me that we as humans need to connect through shared experiences. And that such a simple thing as a *"Butterfly Hug"* can connect two strangers to a moment of Joy!

In the story, Grandma and Becky Jo didn't hurry through their visit.
While they spent time together, they connected not only with words but also through their hearts. Their special moment in the garden became a *"Butterfly Hug"* that would connect them to each other throughout this life and beyond.

ACKNOWLEDGMENTS

Some Additional "Butterfly Hugs" to some very special people:

SPECIAL THANKS TO:

My parents, Don & Phyllis Robbins…
I will be forever thankful to both of you for the unconditional love
and guidance that you gave to me throughout my life.

My Family: Marvin, Matt & Alison, Haley & Nicole and Kelly & Andrew…
Because of you, God instilled in me a passion
to share "Legacy Lessons" from my heart.
I love you all very much!

Ron Mazellan, who encouraged me to keep moving this story forward…
Pastor Jamie Hart, and Joe Casteneda who encouraged me to keep on writing.
*God strategically placed each of you in my life throughout the years as I have taken small
but determined steps towards "writing with His Purpose In Mind"…*

Connie Gorrell, Dennis Kirchner and Lisa Hardwick-Peplow who God used in a subtle…
yet mighty way to give me the confidence that I needed to
move this story forward into a published work.
*Thank you all for the words of encouragement that you gave me
at a very crucial fork in the road to publishing.*

Troy DeLacy Cleland who has a passion for sharing Christ
with children of all ages through his talents.
It has been an honor and a pleasure to work on this project with you!

Gail & Brynne, two delightful ladies
who made my first professional photo shoots a lot of FUN! *Thank you!*
Amanda Savick & Ruth Miller, who in separate, brief encounters,
unknowingly encouraged me to keep writing.

Linda Garber who in fulfilling her dreams became an inspiration for me to pursue mine.

MY THOUGHTS:

*I believe that God allows people to strategically enter our lives for His Purpose
when we have a heart that is seeking to do His Will.*

*I thank God for each of you as you have become a part of my life's journey.
To God Be The Glory for His Amazing Timing and Design.*

Beth* Robbins Bontrager

Author Bio:

Beth Robbins Bontrager, originally from Marion, IN, moved to Goshen Indiana after marrying Marvin Bontrager in 1975. She is the mother of two children, both now married, Matt (Alison) and Kelly (Andrew) and the grandmother of two granddaughters: Haley and Nicole.

As a Mother and Junior Church Teacher, Beth has been in tune with the hearts of children for many years. Now, as a Grandmother, her passion to share "Legacy Lessons" which she has acquired in her lifetime, with children of all ages has surfaced in her first book "Butterfly Hugs".

Throughout her "Stories from a Grandmother's Heart", Beth uses direct and indirect insights from God's Word because she feels that in our ever changing world, it is God's unchanging Truth that can give children as well as adults, stability, encouragement and the renewed hope to live life to its fullest.

Illustrator Bio:

Troy Cleland is originally from Gambier Ohio. He grew up in the country playing down by the "crick" with his little brother Josh and loves the simple life. Troy is married to his wife of 15 years, Melissa and they have a beautiful daughter named Aslinn and an extremely devoted and rambunctious chocolate lab named Piper. Troy and his family currently live in Niles, Michigan where he works as the Operations Manager at Michiana Christian Service Camp. Troy hopes to continue his passion for art where ever it may lead him.

May God receive all the Glory.